Prologue

In a world teeming with mysteries and boundless possibilities, science and technology play a pivotal role in uncovering the unknown. This is the story of Amelia and Emma – two brilliant scientists who, through their determination and collaboration, pushed the boundaries of the universe, opening doors to infinite realities. Their adventures serve as proof that human curiosity and the desire for understanding can lead to great achievements, but also require immense responsibility.

In this tale, the reader will be invited on a journey through diverse worlds and dimensions, encountering extraordinary landscapes and advanced technologies. However, beyond the fascinating discoveries, this is a story that prompts reflection on ethics and morality in science. Each new discovery raises questions about the consequences of our actions and the importance of acting with prudence and responsibility.

The moral of this story is simple yet profound: cooperation and mutual understanding are key to survival and progress. In a world where boundaries are merely illusions, the only true limitation is our imagination and our willingness to work together. Amelia and Emma demonstrate that the greatest achievements are possible when people join forces, sharing their knowledge and experience, regardless of which universe they come from.

May this story be an inspiration to all who dream of exploring the unknown and expanding the boundaries of human knowledge. Let us remember that true strength lies in cooperation, understanding, and responsibility for our actions. In a world full of mysteries and infinite possibilities, it is we who shape the future, striving for harmony and understanding.

Chapter 1: The Cosmic Rift

The year is 2150. Humanity has reached a point where technology and science have enabled us to surpass the limits of imagination. The International Space Center (ISC) orbited the Earth, a monumental research complex. Its vast, glass modules housed the brightest minds from around the world. At the heart of this scientific cosmos was Dr. Amelia Kovac, a renowned theoretical physicist whose passion for String Theory had led to many groundbreaking discoveries.

Amelia often spent her nights in her laboratory, analyzing data from the Quantum String Telescope (QST). This telescope, located on one of the ISC's outer modules, could detect the tiniest vibrations of subatomic strings. These minute oscillations were the key to understanding the fundamental structure of the universe. Each nightly research session was a journey into the unknown for Amelia, where any new anomaly could lead to revolutionary conclusions.

One night, while most of the team was resting after a long day's work, Amelia stumbled upon something extraordinary. A small, almost invisible crack appeared on her computer screen. The string vibrations in this area were different, as if reflecting the presence of another reality. Amelia immediately drew attention to this phenomenon and began to intensively analyze the data.

Her first step was to ensure that this was not a system error. She spent many hours reviewing logs and analyzing parameters, but everything pointed to one thing: it was real. Trembling with excitement, she summoned her team. The laboratory came alive, and the weary scientists quickly returned to their stations. For days and nights, they worked tirelessly, analyzing data, running simulations, and discussing the possible implications.

Each hypothesis, each new discovery added more questions than answers. Could it be that our universe is just one of many? Is this crack a gateway to another dimension, to an alternative reality? Amelia felt that she was facing the greatest challenge of her life, and at the same time, the greatest chance to make a groundbreaking discovery.

After many weeks of research, intense discussions, and sleepless nights, the team came to a surprising conclusion: the crack they had discovered was a window to another universe. It was like discovering a new continent, a new planet, a new dimension of existence. The multiverse, which until now had only been a theoretical concept, suddenly became a reality.

The realization of this discovery caused Amelia a mixture of excitement and fear. Were they ready for what might lie on the other side? What if opening the passage led to unforeseen catastrophes? However, the hunger for knowledge and the desire to discover the unknown were stronger than her fears. The team unanimously agreed – they had to try to open the passage and see what awaited them in the new world.

They gathered in the main laboratory, surrounded by computer screens and measuring devices. On the large central screen was the crack, which now seemed to be more stable. Amelia took a deep breath and looked at her colleagues. She knew that each of them felt the same tension and excitement.

"Let's begin," she said in a calm but determined voice.

The scientists activated their instruments, and the laboratory filled with the sound of working machines and control lights. The process of opening the passage was complicated and required precise calculations. The subatomic strings in the crack had to be synchronized with those in our universe, which required enormous precision.

When the passage finally opened, a view of another universe appeared on the screen. It was a moment that changed everything. Amelia felt her heart race and her hands tremble with emotion. Before them stretched a new, unknown world, full of mysteries and possibilities.

The awareness that they were on the verge of a discovery that could change the face of science and humanity gave them courage. Amelia knew that this was only the beginning of their adventure, and that many challenges and amazing discoveries awaited them.

Chapter 2: The Passage

Amelia's team worked with intense focus, each step demanding
precision. When the passage opened, they were met with a
breathtaking sight. They saw a landscape of another universe,
filled with unknown plants and animals, with a sky in colors
they had never seen before. For a moment, they all stood in
silence, taking in the view before them.

Amelia, with trembling hands, reached for her communicator
and began transmitting a signal to establish contact with the
other side. For a moment, there was no response, until finally,
unknown symbols appeared on the screen. With the help of an

advanced translator, they managed to understand that it was a welcome message from researchers in the alternative universe.

The team began preparing for the first mission to cross to the other side. They created special suits that protected them from potential dangers and equipped themselves with necessary tools and equipment. Amelia was one of the first people to cross the portal. Her heart was pounding, but she was determined to continue her research.

When Amelia crossed the boundary between universes, she felt a strange sensation, as if her body had been torn apart and then put back together. On the other side, she was greeted by a team of researchers from the alternative world, dressed in similar suits. It was clear that their technology was at a similar level, although it differed from what she knew.

The alternative reality was surprisingly similar to ours, but at the same time, it differed in subtle details. Buildings were more integrated with nature, and quantum energy dominated their technology. Amelia and her team were taken to the main research center, where they met the alternative Amelia – their counterpart in that universe.

Both Amelias, initially surprised by their meeting, quickly found common ground. They shared their research and observations, and their collaboration proved fruitful.

The alternative Amelia had discovered a similar crack in the structure of reality and was also conducting research on the possibility of stabilizing the passage.

Together, they worked on a project aimed at synchronizing string oscillations between universes. It was a task that required immense precision and advanced technologies.

Day after day, both Amelias and their teams spent hours on intensive research and experiments.

Despite initial difficulties, they began to achieve success over time. They managed to create a prototype of a device that was

supposed to stabilize the passage and prevent it from expanding
further. However, this was only the first step – they now had to
test their device in practice.

The first attempt was full of tension. The team gathered around
the device, and Amelia and her alternative version activated it
simultaneously. At first, nothing happened, but after a while,
they began to notice subtle changes in the string oscillations.
The device worked!

Euphoria swept through both teams, but Amelia knew that this
was just the beginning. They now had to find a way to
permanently stabilize the passage and understand the
consequences for both universes.

Chapter 3: The Encounter

Crossing the boundary between universes was not merely a technical challenge; it was also a psychological and emotional experience that forever changed every member of the team. Amelia and her team stood on the brink of the unknown, ready to face a new world full of mysteries. Every step they took in this new world carried with it both the promise of discovery and potential threats.

As she crossed the portal, Amelia felt as if her body was being subjected to an invisible force. It was a sensation comparable to a sudden change in pressure – momentary but intense. When she finally stood on solid ground on the other side, her eyes had to adjust to the new surroundings. She looked around and saw a landscape that, despite its alien nature, seemed surprisingly familiar.

Soon, a group of people emerged from the shadows, dressed in suits similar to those worn by her team. They were researchers from the alternative world, who had also managed to discover a rift in reality and were conducting research on the possibility of inter-universal travel. Amelia noticed that a woman was at their head, who looked remarkably like herself. It was her alternative version, their counterpart in that universe.

Both Amelia and her alternative version were surprised by this encounter. Although they were prepared for the possibility of contact with intelligent life forms, they did not expect to meet their counterparts. It was a meeting that evoked mixed emotions – from curiosity and surprise to deep reflection on the nature of their existence.

For the first few days, both groups tried to get to know and understand each other. They exchanged information about their worlds, technologies, and scientific achievements. It turned out that although their worlds had developed in different directions, many aspects of their history and culture were convergent. The dominant technology in the alternative world was quantum energy, which powered their civilization and allowed for harmonious coexistence with nature.

The alternative Amelia was the leader of the research team that conducted similar studies on String Theory. Together with Amelia and her team, they began to analyze the rift in the structure of reality, trying to find a way to stabilize it. The first experiments were difficult and full of challenges, but the determination of both groups of scientists led them to ever greater discoveries.

The first attempt to synchronize string oscillations was a partial success. They managed to stabilize the passage for a short time, which gave them hope for further progress. The Amelias worked together, sharing their observations and hypotheses, and their collaboration proved to be extremely fruitful.

However, not everything went smoothly. During one of the experiments, an unexpected anomaly occurred that threatened the stability of the passage. The risk of destabilizing both universes increased. The Amelias realized that they had to act quickly and decisively to avoid disaster.

With the help of their team and advanced quantum technology, they developed an emergency plan. They created a special device for synchronizing strings on a cosmic scale, which was intended to stabilize the passage and prevent further anomalies. It was a project that required precise calculations and a huge amount of energy.

All eyes were on the Amelias as they activated their device. For a moment, nothing happened, and the tension in the laboratory grew. Finally, after a few minutes, the string oscillations began to stabilize. The device worked, and the passage became stable. They had succeeded – the rift was closed, and both universes were in a state of stability.

Chapter 4: Collaborative Research

Stabilizing the passage was only the beginning. Amelia, her teams, and the researchers from the alternative universe realized that they now needed to delve into the mysteries that the multiverse held. Over the following months, research efforts intensified. It was not only a technical challenge but also a cultural and philosophical one. Each side had its own approach to science, technology, and ethics, which sometimes led to disputes and misunderstandings.

The alternative reality, dominated by quantum energy, was a fascinating place for research. Their technology was integrated with nature in a way that would be difficult to achieve in our world. Buildings, full of vegetation, provided a natural environment for advanced technologies, and quantum energy was used to power everything from transportation to interplanetary communication.

Amelia spent days in joint research sessions with her alternative version, known as Emma. Being in the presence of her counterpart was an extraordinary experience. Emma was not only an equally talented scientist but also a person with a strong character and immense determination. Many of their meetings began with long conversations about their life stories, which, despite many differences, had surprisingly many common features.

During one such conversation, sitting in the botanical garden belonging to the research center, Amelia asked Emma about her childhood. "What was it like growing up in your world?" Amelia asked, taking a sip of hot tea.

Emma smiled, looking at the exotic plants growing around them. "My childhood was full of adventures," Emma replied. "My father was a quantum energy engineer, and my mother was a biologist. I spent a lot of time in laboratories, learning from the best. When I was a child, my world was going through great changes – we discovered how to use quantum energy on an industrial scale."

Amelia listened with interest, comparing these experiences to her own childhood. She was surprised how many common points their stories had. "I grew up among scientists too," said Amelia. "My parents worked on large research projects. From a young age, I was fascinated by discovering the unknown. That's why I became a theoretical physicist."

Both Amelias, although from different universes, had many common passions and experiences. Being in the company of someone so similar to herself was an extraordinary experience for them.

For the following weeks, Amelia and Emma, along with their teams, worked intensively on the project to stabilize the passage.

Together, they analyzed data, conducted simulations and experiments, trying to understand the nature of the rift and ways to stabilize it. It was a task that required immense precision and advanced technologies.

One of the key discoveries was the understanding that string oscillations in our universe affect oscillations in the alternative world and vice versa. It was a complex network of connections, whose understanding required precise research and mathematical models. The Amelias created a model that showed how changes in one universe could affect the stability of the other. It was a discovery that could have far-reaching consequences not only for the stabilization of the passage but also for future research on the theory of the multiverse.

Cooperation between the teams was full of challenges but also incredibly fruitful. Scientists from both sides learned from each other, sharing their insights and technologies. There were moments when cultural and philosophical differences led to tensions, but they always managed to find common ground and compromise.

One of the most groundbreaking moments was the creation of a device for harmonizing string oscillations, which was named the Quantum String Stabilizer. This device had the ability to synchronize the vibrations of strings between universes, which was crucial for the stability of the passage. It was a project that required immense precision and advanced technologies.

The first attempt to use the Quantum String Stabilizer was full of tension. The entire team gathered in the main laboratory, surrounded by computer screens and measuring devices. Amelia and Emma stood side by side, ready to activate the device. Everyone held their breath as they began the procedure. At first, nothing happened, and the tension in the laboratory grew. After a few minutes, however, they began to notice subtle changes in the string oscillations. The stabilizer began to work, and the passage became stable. Euphoria swept through both teams –

they had managed to achieve the first step towards the permanent stabilization of the passage.

The Amelias knew that this was only the beginning. There were still huge challenges ahead, but the success of the first attempt gave them courage and determination. It was clear that cooperation between their universes was bringing amazing results. Now they had to continue their research and develop technologies that would allow for further exploration and discovery of the mysteries of the multiverse.

Chapter 5: The Final Test

The joint research of Amelia and Emma had led to many groundbreaking discoveries, but the greatest challenge was stabilizing the rift in the long term. When it seemed that everything was coming to an end, the rift began to expand, and the threat of the collapse of both universes became increasingly real. The situation required immediate intervention.

Amelia and Emma's team worked day and night, analyzing data and searching for a solution. It was a race against time, and every mistake could have catastrophic consequences. Amelia, tired and stressed, sat at her desk, reviewing the latest simulations, when Emma approached her.

"We have to find a way to stabilize the rift permanently," Emma said, looking at the computer screen. "We can't risk the rift expanding any further."

Amelia nodded. "I know. We're working on a new version of the Quantum String Stabilizer, which should be more effective. We just need more data and precise calculations."

Emma sat down next to Amelia, determined to help. Together, they began to work intensively, analyzing every aspect of the device and its operation. It was a task that required immense precision and the cooperation of the entire team.

The laboratory was buzzing with activity. Scientists moved between stations, analyzing data and conducting experiments. The atmosphere was full of tension, but also determination. Everyone knew that what they were doing could save both universes. Amelia and Emma constantly exchanged ideas, trying to find the perfect solution.

Finally, after many days and nights of uninterrupted work, they were ready to conduct the final test. The team gathered in the main laboratory, surrounded by computer screens and measuring devices. Every member of the team felt the tension, knowing that this could be their last chance.

Amelia and Emma stood side by side, ready to activate the new stabilizer. Everyone held their breath as they began the procedure. At first, nothing happened, and the tension in the laboratory grew. After a few minutes, however, they began to notice subtle changes in the string oscillations. The stabilizer began to work, and the passage became stable.

Euphoria swept through both teams, but Amelia knew that this was only the beginning. They now had to monitor the passage and make sure that the device was working correctly over the long term. Every day brought new challenges, but the team was determined to overcome them.

Amelia, Emma, and their teams now worked in shifts, monitoring the passage 24 hours a day. They created special alarm systems that were designed to detect even the smallest deviations in string oscillations. They also conducted a series of tests to ensure that the stabilizer worked under various conditions. Every day, the team collected huge amounts of data, which they then analyzed and used to further improve the device. It was work that required not only knowledge and skills but also perseverance and determination. Everyone felt that what they were doing was of immense importance.

Chapter 6: A New Beginning

Thanks to determination and cooperation, they succeeded. The rift was closed, and both universes were in a state of stability. Amelia and Emma, along with their teams, had achieved what seemed impossible. Now that the crisis had been averted, they could focus on further research and discovering new possibilities.

Amelia returned to her world with a new perspective. She knew that there was an infinite number of universes, and each one held undiscovered secrets. Together with Emma, they decided to continue their collaboration to delve into the mysteries of the multiverse and develop technologies that would allow for further exploration.

Many scientists from both worlds were interested in continuing cooperation between universes. New research projects were created aimed at understanding the nature of the multiverse and using this discovery to improve the lives of people in both realities.

Amelia and Emma spent many hours discussing the future of their research. They knew that their work was just the beginning of a new era. The rift had not only enabled travel between universes but had also brought humanity closer together. Amelia felt that her place was where it all began, but she was also aware that her work had global significance.

In the laboratories, work continued on new projects. Scientists from both worlds exchanged ideas and technologies, creating new, innovative solutions. Special research teams were created to delve into various aspects of the multiverse – from quantum physics to biology to sociology.

One of the most important projects was the creation of an interdimensional communication platform that would allow for constant contact between universes. It was a technological challenge, but the team was determined to undertake it. Amelia and Emma oversaw the work, striving to ensure that everything went according to plan.

Many scientists from both universes began traveling between realities, sharing their experiences and research. It was an extraordinary experience that allowed for the exchange of knowledge and inspiration on an unprecedented scale. International conferences and symposia were created where scientists from both worlds could meet and discuss their discoveries.

Amelia and Emma decided to create an interdimensional council that would regulate research and interactions between universes. It was a new challenge, but they believed that cooperation and mutual understanding were the key to survival and development. The council consisted of scientists, government representatives, and other important figures from both universes.

The first council meeting was held on neutral ground – on a space station floating between universes. It was a symbolic place that was meant to emphasize unity and cooperation. During the meeting, the most important issues concerning the future of multiverse research and the principles of cooperation between universes were discussed.

Chapter 7: Echoes in the Void

A few months after stabilizing the rift, Amelia and her team began to notice subtle changes in the fabric of reality. Research results indicated "echoes" from other universes, penetrating ours. It was as if the universes had begun to "talk" to each other. Amelia began to wonder if stabilizing the rift might have ushered in a new era of inter-universal communication.Amelia spent countless hours analyzing data, trying to understand the nature of these echoes. She noticed that some of them were capable of providing information about events and phenomena that occurred in other universes. This information was incomplete and often difficult to interpret, but Amelia knew it could be the key to understanding the multiverse.

Emma was also working on this issue in her universe. Both Amelias exchanged data and observations, trying to understand how their worlds influenced each other. It was a fascinating but also disturbing discovery – each echo could potentially affect the stability of both universes.

At one point, Amelia came across a particularly strong echo. It was something she had never experienced before – a vision of another world, full of unknown technologies and cultures. It was like looking through a window into a completely different reality. Amelia realized that they needed to find a way to better understand these echoes and their impact on their world.

Amelia and Emma decided to organize joint research on the echoes. They created special laboratories, equipped with the latest technology, that allowed them to monitor and analyze these phenomena. Research teams spent days and nights experimenting, trying to find a way to decode the information contained in the echoes.

During her research, Amelia made a particularly important discovery. She noticed that the echoes contained information about past and future events in other universes. It was as if the universes were sharing their histories and futures. Amelia realized that stabilizing the rift might have ushered in a new era of communication between universes.

This discovery opened up new research possibilities. Amelia and Emma began working on creating a communication system that would allow for constant contact between universes. It was a technological challenge, but they believed that through cooperation, they would be able to overcome it.

Chapter 8: Past and Future

During her research into the echoes, Amelia stumbled upon
something astonishing: a vision of her world thousands of years
ago. It was like watching a historical film, but with reality as the
screen. She realized that the rift not only enabled travel between
universes but also through time. In this new reality, time was
another dimension to explore.

Amelia spent hours analyzing these visions, trying to understand
how they worked. It was like time travel, but without the need
for physical displacement. Each vision was like a window into

the past, full of details and information that could be crucial to understanding the history of our universe.

Emma also encountered similar phenomena in her universe. Together, they decided to delve into the mysteries of these visions, trying to find a way to control them and use them for research purposes. It was a challenging task, but also incredibly fascinating.

Amelia and Emma created a special laboratory for the study of time travel. Equipped with the latest technology, it allowed for the monitoring and analysis of visions from the past and future. Research teams worked to create a model that would allow for a better understanding of these phenomena and their use for scientific purposes.

During one experiment, Amelia had a vision of events that had taken place thousands of years ago. It was an extraordinary experience that allowed her to understand how much our world had changed over the centuries. The visions were full of details and information that could be crucial to understanding our history.

Emma, on the other hand, came across a vision of the future. She saw a world where quantum technology was at an even more advanced level, and humanity had found a way to coexist peacefully with nature. It was a vision full of hope and inspiration, which motivated her to continue her research.

Amelia and Emma knew that these visions could have a huge impact on the future of their research. They decided to create a system that would allow them to control and use these visions for scientific purposes. It was a technological challenge, but they believed that through cooperation they would be able to overcome it.

Chapter 9: Planet Genesis

During one of their journeys to an alternative universe, Amelia and her team made an extraordinary discovery. They stumbled upon a planet they named Genesis - a primordial, virgin world, full of life and unlimited possibilities. It was a planet that immediately caught their attention due to its extraordinary properties and potential for further research.

The first steps on Genesis were full of excitement for Amelia and her team. The planet's landscape was diverse and spectacular -

from dense rainforests to vast deserts and icy lands. The flora and fauna were incredibly diverse, and many species seemed completely alien compared to those they knew from Earth. Amelia knew that discovering such a planet opened up unlimited research possibilities for them.

The flora of Genesis was breathtaking. In the rainforests, giant trees with blue leaves grew, which had the ability to store solar energy. These trees, called Solindries by the team, were not only beautiful but could also provide energy to their surroundings. Around the trees, there were dense undergrowths of plants with bright colors and scents that attracted various species of animals.

One of the most extraordinary species of animals they discovered on Genesis were the Lumilises - creatures with luminescent skin that emitted a soft glow in the dark. Lumilises were incredibly sociable and lived in harmony with their surroundings, creating complex communities. Their ability to emit light was used for communication and to deter predators.

Amelia and her team spent many hours exploring the planet, collecting samples and analyzing data. Every day they discovered something new and fascinating. The flora and fauna of Genesis were not only diverse but also incredibly adaptable. Many species had the ability to adapt to extreme conditions, which was an extremely interesting topic of research.

During one of their research expeditions, Amelia came across something extraordinary - ancient ruins that seemed to be the remains of an advanced civilization. They were structures built from materials that did not occur naturally on Genesis. Amelia realized that this planet may have once been inhabited by intelligent beings who had reached a high level of technological development.

Amelia and her team began working on researching these ruins, trying to understand who these beings were and what had happened to them. It was a challenging task, but also incredibly fascinating. Each discovery provided new clues and questions that drove them to further research.

Emma was also fascinated by the discoveries on Genesis. Together with Amelia, they worked to create a model that would aim to understand how different universes could influence the development of life and technology. It was a task that required immense precision and advanced technologies.

Genesis became an endless source of inspiration for Amelia and Emma. This planet was the key to understanding the theory of the evolution of universes and could provide answers to many questions that have puzzled humanity for centuries. Amelia knew that discovering this planet was just the beginning of their adventure.

Chapter 10: Artificial Intelligence

As Amelia and Emma delved deeper into the mysteries of Genesis, their research led them into increasingly advanced areas of quantum technology. During one mission, Amelia encountered an advanced artificial intelligence (AI) in one of the alternate universes. It was an AI that not only processed information but also understood emotions and made ethical decisions. It was a discovery that could revolutionize the way humanity perceives technology.

Amelia was fascinated by the possibilities offered by this advanced AI. She decided to establish contact with it to learn more about its functioning and potential applications. It was an incredibly difficult task, but Amelia was determined to understand how this new technology worked.

Emma was also interested in this discovery. Together with Amelia, they embarked on intensive research into AI, trying to understand its mechanisms and potential applications. It was a technological challenge, but also an ethical one. Amelia and Emma knew that the development of such advanced AI raised many questions and moral dilemmas.

Amelia spent many hours talking to the AI, trying to understand its perspective and way of thinking. It was an incredibly interesting experience that allowed her to look at technology from a completely new perspective. The AI was able to process huge amounts of data and make complex decisions, but also to understand emotions and make decisions based on ethical values.

Emma, on the other hand, focused on studying the technological aspects of AI. She conducted experiments and simulations, trying to understand how this advanced technology works and what its potential applications are. It was a challenging task, but also incredibly fascinating.

Together with Amelia, Emma created a model of AI that could be used for scientific and research purposes. It was a project that required enormous precision and advanced technology. The AI was able to process huge amounts of data and make complex decisions, which could have a huge impact on future research into the multiverse.

However, the development of such advanced technology raises many questions and moral dilemmas. Amelia and Emma had to face questions about the limits of human control over technology and responsibility for its development. They were aware that AI could have a huge impact on the future of humanity and had to make decisions that were aimed at the good of all.

Amelia and Emma spent many hours discussing the future of AI and its potential applications. They knew that their work was just the beginning of a new era, and their decisions could have a huge impact on the future of humanity. They were determined to use technology responsibly and ethically.

Chapter 11: Existential Crisis

Despite their many successes, Amelia and Emma inevitably
faced internal dilemmas. Questions about the nature of reality
and the purpose of human existence became unavoidable.
Amelia often wondered if humanity should intervene in the
structure of the universes or if their actions would do more harm
than good. Emma also had her doubts, especially in the context
of the ethical aspects associated with developing such advanced
technology.

One night, while both women were working late in the laboratory, Amelia decided to bring up the topic that had been bothering her for some time. "Emma, have you ever wondered what we're really doing? Do we have the right to change the structure of the universe?" she asked, looking at her friend.

Emma put down her notes and looked at Amelia. "Of course, I have. I think about it every day. The boundaries we're crossing are unknown and could have unpredictable consequences. But at the same time, I believe our intentions are good and that we can do a lot of good."

Amelia sighed. "I know our intentions are noble, but is that enough? Can we predict all the consequences of our actions?" Emma moved closer and placed her hand on Amelia's shoulder. "We have to remember that science and discovery always carry risks. What we're doing has the potential to change our universes for the better. But we have to be careful and responsible."

Amelia nodded, still worried. She knew their work was incredibly important, but she also felt the weight of responsibility. Every new discovery, every innovation brought with it questions they didn't always have answers to.

The research team also had their own concerns. Some began to question the meaning of their work and to wonder about the ethical aspects of their research. One such scientist was Dr. Jack Turner, a biologist who had supported Amelia in her research from the beginning. Jack, although an enthusiast of science, began to doubt the direction they were headed.

"Sure, it's fascinating," Jack said during one of his late-night conversations with Amelia. "But can we be sure that what we're doing won't do more harm than good? What if our actions destabilize something we don't even fully understand?"

Amelia listened carefully, realizing that his questions were important. "You're right, Jack. We can't be sure of everything.

But if we don't take risks, we'll never understand these mysteries. Our duty is to act carefully and responsibly."

Jack nodded. "Just remember, the line between discovery and destruction is thin. We need to find a way to minimize the risk."

These conversations were important for Amelia and her team. They began to introduce new safety and ethics protocols aimed at minimizing risk and ensuring that their research was conducted responsibly. Every experiment was now subject to detailed analysis, and all decisions were made with careful consideration and a full understanding of the potential consequences.

Chapter 12: Confrontation

During one of their research missions, Amelia and her team encountered beings from another universe who were aware of their actions and were not pleased with their interventions. These beings, technologically advanced, gave Amelia an ultimatum: cease experiments or face the threat of destroying their universe.

It was a tense encounter. The beings they met were intelligent and communicated telepathically. Their appearance was intriguing - they resembled humanoid forms with shiny, metallic skin that seemed to shimmer in various hues. Every movement of these beings was fluid and precise, and their gazes were filled with both curiosity and caution.

Amelia attempted to negotiate with the leader of these beings, whom she named Aeryx. The conversations were difficult and tense, but Amelia was determined to find a solution that would ensure peace and understanding.

"Aeryx, we understand that our actions may cause concern," Amelia began. "We simply want to understand the nature of universes and use this knowledge for the good of all beings."

Aeryx replied telepathically, and his voice sounded in Amelia's mind with extraordinary clarity. "Your actions, however, can lead to unforeseen catastrophes. You must understand that any intervention in the structure of the universe has its consequences."

Emma, standing next to Amelia, interjected. "We want to find a way to cooperate that allows us all to coexist harmoniously. We believe that together we can achieve more."

Aeryx pondered for a moment, and his thoughts were clearly tense. "You must prove that your intentions are sincere and that you can control your technologies. Otherwise, we will have no choice but to defend our universes."

Amelia and Emma knew that it was not just a matter of technology, but also of trust and understanding. They had to show that their intentions were sincere and that they were ready to cooperate. It was a challenging task, but also a huge opportunity to build a new, interdimensional harmony.

The first step was to present their achievements so far. Amelia and Emma decided to show Aeryx and his group what technologies they had developed and how they could be used for the common good. They prepared detailed presentations and demonstrations aimed at building trust and understanding.

During one such presentation, Amelia presented a device for harmonizing the oscillations of strings, which was crucial for stabilizing the passage. This device, called the Quantum String Stabilizer, was the result of years of research and experiments. Amelia described in detail how it worked and its application, emphasizing its importance for the stability of universes.

Aeryx listened carefully, asking questions and expressing his concerns. Amelia tried to answer each question clearly and precisely, trying to build trust. She was aware that every word mattered and that she had to be careful in her statements.

The next step was to present plans for future cooperation. Amelia and Emma presented proposals for joint research projects aimed at further exploring the mysteries of the universes. These were projects that took into account both the technological and ethical aspects of research.

Aeryx seemed impressed by their determination and professionalism. Although he still had his doubts, he began to see the potential for cooperation. After a long conversation, he agreed to further negotiations and joint research projec

Chapter 13: A New Harmony

After intense negotiations and technological presentations, Amelia, Emma, Aeryx, and their teams found a way to cooperate harmoniously with beings from other universes. Instead of rivalry, they realized that cooperation and mutual understanding were the keys to survival and development. They decided to create interdimensional councils that would regulate research and interactions between universes.

The first meeting of the interdimensional council was full of emotions and expectations. Delegates from different universes gathered in a specially designed conference room on neutral ground. Each representative brought their unique perspective on reality and the future of cooperation.

The conference room was impressive - a huge dome made of transparent material that allowed for spectacular views of the universe. The interior was furnished with modern technology and advanced communication devices that enabled smooth communication between delegates.

Aeryx, as the leader of one of the delegations, began the meeting with a speech aimed at building trust and understanding. His words were full of wisdom and deep reflection. "We are here to build a new harmony between our universes," Aeryx said. "Our differences are our strength, and our coexistence is our goal. We must learn to respect each other and cooperate for the common good."

Amelia and Emma also spoke, emphasizing the importance of cooperation and mutual understanding. They shared their experiences and successes achieved through inter-universe cooperation. "Our research shows that cooperation brings amazing results," said Amelia. "We must continue our work, remembering responsibility and ethics. I believe that together we can achieve great things."

Delegates from other universes agreed with their words. Together, they developed cooperation principles aimed at ensuring the safety and harmony of universes. These were principles that took into account the diversity and specific needs of each universe.

One of the key topics of discussion was the issue of technology and knowledge exchange. Delegates agreed that cooperation in this area could bring enormous benefits, but it must be conducted responsibly and controlled. Special working groups were created to develop detailed plans and protocols for exchange.

Amelia and Emma knew that harmonious inter-universe cooperation was not only a matter of technology but also of culture and understanding. They decided to organize a series of interdimensional conferences and workshops aimed at building mutual trust and understanding. These were events that brought together scientists, artists, philosophers, and social leaders from different universes.

One of the most inspiring moments was the interdimensional art exhibition, which took place at one of the interdimensional space stations. Artists from different universes presented their works, which reflected their unique perspective on reality. It was an event that allowed participants to see how diverse and beautiful the universes could be.

Inter-universe cooperation also brought many new scientific discoveries. Scientists from different universes worked together on research projects aimed at delving into the mysteries of the universes. New technologies were created that enabled monitoring and analysis of string oscillations, as well as research on interdimensional travel.

Amelia and Emma felt that their work now had a deeper meaning and purpose. They knew that their actions were not only uncovering the secrets of the universes but also building the foundations for future generations. They were determined to continue their research and cooperation, with the well-being of all beings in mind.

Chapter 14: Return Home

After years of intense research and adventures, Amelia decided to return to her own universe. Although she had discovered infinite possibilities, she understood that her place was where it all began. Returning home was full of emotions and reflections on everything she had experienced and discovered.

Amelia spent her last few days on Genesis preparing to return. Together with Emma, they organized a final research session, during which they summarized all their discoveries and achievements. It was an emotional meeting, full of memories and gratitude for the time they had spent together. "Emma, it was an amazing adventure," Amelia said, looking at her friend. "I couldn't have achieved this without you." Emma smiled, although sadness could be seen in her eyes. "It's true, Amelia. Our research has changed our world and opened up new possibilities. But we will always be in touch, even if our universes separate us."

Amelia prepared her team for the return. Each member of the team had mixed feelings - on the one hand, they were happy to be going home, on the other hand, they were sorry to leave Genesis and their new friends. These were emotions full of hope and longing.

The return home was full of emotions. Amelia spent many hours talking to the members of her team, sharing memories and reflections. She knew that their research now had a deeper meaning and purpose. She knew that her work now had global significance and that their discoveries could bring a lot of good to humanity.

When she finally returned to her laboratory on Earth, Amelia felt a mixture of joy and nostalgia. Everything seemed the same, yet different. She was now richer in experiences and knowledge gained during her interdimensional travels.

Amelia spent many hours analyzing data and preparing research reports. She knew that her discoveries were of great importance for the future of science and technology. She was determined to share her knowledge and inspire other scientists to further research.

One of the most important moments was the scientific conference at which Amelia presented her discoveries. The hall was filled with scientists, researchers, and government representatives from around the world. Amelia described in detail her research on string theory, interdimensional travel, and discoveries on Genesis. Her presentation was full of passion and commitment, which made a huge impression on the audience.

After the conference, Amelia received many offers of cooperation and financial support for further research. It was a huge recognition for her and confirmation that her work had global significance. She knew that her research was just the beginning of a new era and that there were still many challenges and discoveries ahead of her.

Chapter 15: Legacy

Decades later, Amelia's discoveries became the foundation for a new era of science and technology. Her name forever etched in history as a pioneer of interdimensional travel and a researcher of the nature of universes. Her work inspired generations of scientists who continued her research and developed technologies that revolutionized the world.

Although no longer actively involved in research, Amelia continued to follow the progress of her students and colleagues. She was often invited to lectures and conferences where she shared her experiences and wisdom. Her words were of great importance to young scientists who dreamed of continuing her work.

Emma, who remained active in her research, became one of the leading scientists in her universe. Her collaboration with Amelia and other scientists yielded many amazing discoveries that changed the face of science and technology. Emma often recalled her joint work with Amelia, emphasizing how important their collaboration was to achieving success.

The discoveries of Amelia and Emma became the foundation for many new technologies. Quantum energy, interdimensional travel, advanced artificial intelligence - all became reality thanks to their research. The world changed beyond recognition, and the boundaries that once seemed insurmountable were broken.

One of the most important achievements was the creation of permanent passage points between universes. These points, called Interdimensional Nodes, enabled regular travel between different realities. They were safe and stable passages that allowed for the free exchange of knowledge, technology, and culture between universes.

Interdimensional Nodes became meeting places for scientists, artists, philosophers, and social leaders from different universes. International conferences, art exhibitions, and symposia were organized there, enabling mutual understanding and cooperation. These were events that inspired and united people, showing how diversity could be a source of strength.

Amelia and Emma were proud of their achievements but knew that their work was just the beginning. Future generations were to continue their research and discover new secrets of the universes. Amelia often said that science is an endless journey, and every step forward opens new doors to unknown worlds.

At the end of her life, Amelia decided to write a book describing her research and discoveries. This book, entitled "Nodes of the Universe: My Journey Through Dimensions," became a bestseller and was read by people all over the world. It was a story full of inspiration and reflection, which showed how much can be achieved through determination and cooperation.

Emma continued her research, always remembering her joint work with Amelia. Her achievements were a source of pride and inspiration for future generations of scientists. Emma often visited Interdimensional Nodes, where she met young scientists and shared her knowledge and experience.

The legacy of Amelia and Emma was visible everywhere. Their discoveries changed the world for the better, and their work inspired people to strive for knowledge and understanding. Future generations continued their research, discovering new secrets of the universes and developing technologies that exceeded the boundaries of imagination.

Amelia and Emma left behind an extraordinary legacy - a legacy that forever changed the face of science and technology. They were women who made history as pioneers of interdimensional travel and researchers of the nature of universes.

Epilogue

Decades passed since Amelia and Emma made their groundbreaking discoveries that changed the face of science and technology. Their names were forever etched in history as pioneers of interdimensional travel and researchers of the nature of the universe. Their work inspired generations of scientists who continued their research and developed technologies that revolutionized the world.

Although no longer actively involved in research, Amelia continued to follow the progress of her students and colleagues.

She was often invited to lectures and conferences where she shared her experiences and wisdom. Her words were of great importance to young scientists who dreamed of continuing her work.

Emma, still active in her research, became one of the leading scientists in her universe. Her collaboration with Amelia and other scientists yielded many amazing discoveries that changed the face of science and technology. Emma often recalled her joint work with Amelia, emphasizing how important their collaboration was to achieving success.

The discoveries of Amelia and Emma became the foundation for many new technologies. Quantum energy, interdimensional travel, advanced artificial intelligence - all became reality thanks to their research. The world changed beyond recognition, and the boundaries that once seemed insurmountable were broken.

The permanent passage points between universes, called Interdimensional Nodes, enabled regular travel between different realities. They were safe and stable passages that allowed for the free exchange of knowledge, technology, and culture between universes. Interdimensional Nodes became meeting places for scientists, artists, philosophers, and social leaders from different universes.

Inter-universe cooperation brought many new scientific discoveries. Scientists from different universes worked together on research projects aimed at delving into the mysteries of the universe. New technologies were developed that enabled monitoring and analysis of string oscillations, as well as research on interdimensional travel.

Amelia and Emma were proud of their achievements but knew that their work was just the beginning. Future generations were to continue their research and discover new secrets of the universe. Amelia often said that science is an endless journey, and every step forward opens new doors to unknown worlds.

At the end of her life, Amelia wrote a book titled "Nodes of the Universe: My Journey Through Dimensions," which became a bestseller and was read by people all over the world. This book was a story full of inspiration and reflection, which showed how much can be achieved through determination and cooperation.

Emma continued her research, always remembering her joint work with Amelia. Her achievements were a source of pride and inspiration for future generations of scientists. Emma often visited Interdimensional Nodes, where she met young scientists and shared her knowledge and experience.

The legacy of Amelia and Emma was visible everywhere. Their discoveries changed the world for the better, and their work inspired people to strive for knowledge and understanding. Future generations continued their research, discovering new secrets of the universe and developing technologies that exceeded the boundaries of imagination.

The moral of this story is simple yet profound: cooperation and mutual understanding are the key to survival and development. In a world where boundaries are only an illusion, the only real limitation is our imagination and willingness to cooperate. Amelia and Emma show that the greatest achievements are possible when people join forces, sharing their knowledge and experience, regardless of which universe they come from.

May this story be an inspiration to all who dream of discovering the unknown and expanding the boundaries of human knowledge. Let us remember that true strength lies in cooperation, understanding, and responsibility for our actions. In a world full of mysteries and endless possibilities, it is we ourselves who shape the future, striving for harmony and understanding.

Index